Home Around the Campfire

Written by Stacy Snyder • Illustrated by Anne Johnson

Home Around the Campfire. Ages 3-9.

Text copyright ©2024 by Stacy Snyder. Illustration copyright ©2022 by Anne Johnson.
For information please contact anne@wagdesign.be or stacysnyder@mac.com

First edition: USA 2024 ISBN: 978-0-9600041-8-8

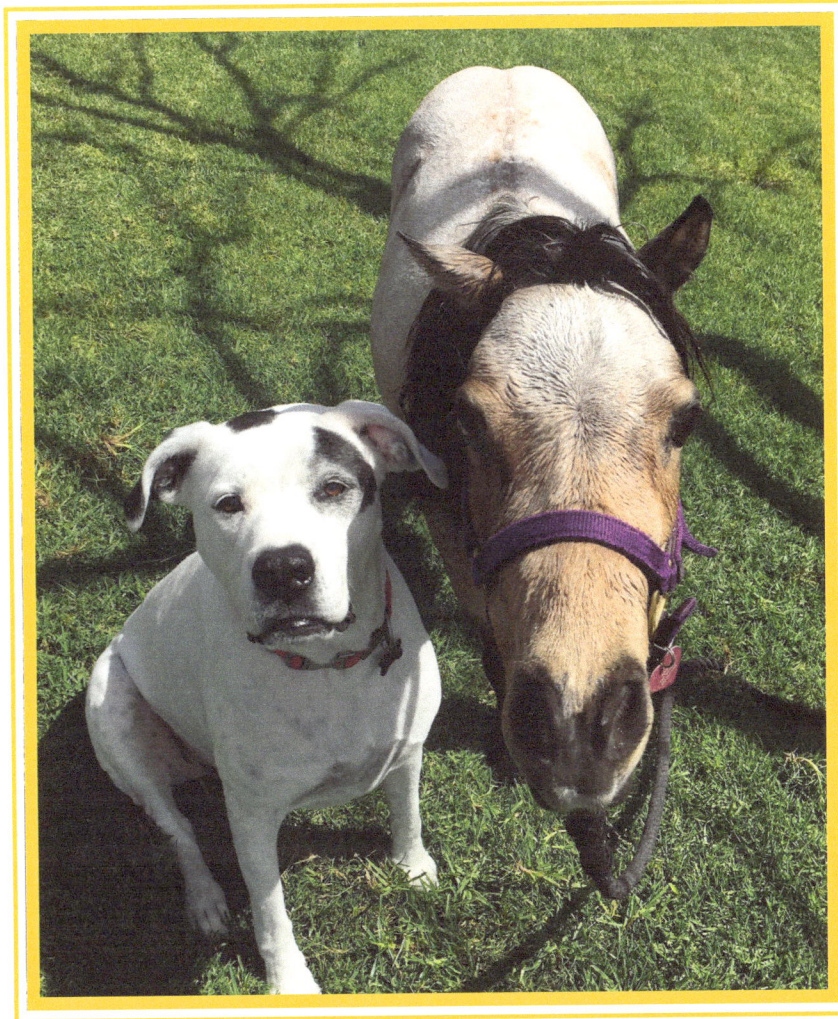

This book is based on the true story
of two rescue animals who found each other
and became Best Friends.

In the morning,
Sticker remembered what the Moon had
said, while he was hiding in the tall grass.
It was about the light rain and a Rainbow
appearing.

As Sticker looked up into the sky, there it was the beautiful Rainbow. That meant it was time to move.

Sticker found a tree stump
and launched himself into the air
to release the latch to the old shed

6

The door opened
and we began galloping
towards the colorful Rainbow.

As my parents and I were running away,
we heard a loud rumble.

It was the Farmer.

—AGAIN!

While Cranky the Crow was quietly bathing,
he heard Henry the Hawk
cry out in the distance,

"Cranky, Please help us!"

Cranky flew away quickly
and moments later...

9

...He appeared with his crew of crows. They surrounded the Farmer and started pecking at the side of the tractor. There were crows everywhere!

The Farmer could not see where he was going—
— and drove straight into a ditch.

My parents and I ran into the forest,
following the magnificent Rainbow.
We walked all day. Finally, just before nightfall,
we saw the magical tree in the distance.

Safely away from the Farmer, we could now rest.

That night when the Moon and Sparkle rose,
we all began to sing—

Thank you, thank you,

For all you do!

You freed us from

The Farmer too!"

The next morning was beautiful.

Birds were singing,

bees were buzzing,

and flowers were blooming.

Henry was flying ahead.

He could see the magical tree and just behind it–

–the house where the Lady in the Red Hat lived.

"We are almost there,"
chirped Henry.

17

As we rounded the tree, we saw the Lady in the Red Hat
watering flowers with Charger. The Lady and Charger looked up—

—and we ran towards each other jumping, clapping, flapping and dancing with delight!

That evening,

— we looked up at the Moon and Sparkle—

— and said, "THANK YOU!"

Days later, while my parents and I were resting,

we heard someone driving down the gravel road.

SUGAR SHACK

Much to our surprise
we saw the Farmer.
We were afraid he had come
to take us back to his old shed.

He got out of his tractor to talk to The Lady in The Red Hat,

who was not happy to see him.

After a long talk with The Farmer, the Lady told me and my parents —

"The Farmer has something he wants to say."

The Farmer bowed his head and said,
"I'm sorry to have scared you. I want to be your friend
and treat you with kindness."

Relieved,
My parents and I invited the Farmer
to stay the evening for a celebration with Sparkle and the Moon.

The new friends gathered that night around the campfire
forming a circle of love while roasting marshmallows and telling stories.

We were so grateful to be together, forever, in our new home.

Life was REALLY good!

FAMILY ♡ MEMORIES ♡

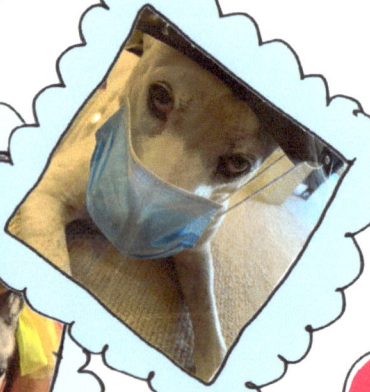

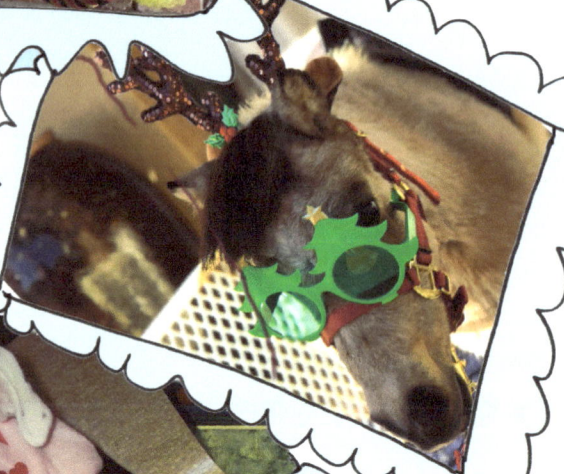

GOOD VIBES!

FRIENDSHIP

Now go back and see if you can spot any of these friendly little creatures.

Housefly

Acorn

Luna moth

Bottlecap

Chipmunk

29

For Charger

Love, Charlie.

30

STACY SNYDER is a graduate of the University of Arizona, with a degree in Special Education. She resides in San Diego California, with her loving husband John. She is the mother of two daughters, and the grandmother of four beautiful grandchildren. Her background in education and love for nature were the inspiration for this book. She was taken by the extraordinary relationship that developed between a rescued dog and a rescued miniature horse. Their unconditional love is a heart-warming example of kindness.

ANNE JOHNSON has held a career in painting, illustration and fine arts for over 30 years. She received a Bachelor of Arts degree from Roanoke College followed by a Master of Arts degree in Medical Illustration from the Medical College of Georgia, now Georgia Health Sciences University. She has an endless love for animals and nature and has been passionate about children's books since she was a young girl. After residing in Belgium for over 25 years she has recently returned to her hometown, Wayzata, Minnesota, and is the proud mother of three loving young adults, two dogs, a cat, and a horse. *Home Around the Campfire* is her fourth book with Stacy Snyder.

SUGAR is a rescued buckskin miniature horse. She was in very poor shape when she was adopted. Scared and very skittish. With patience and spending lots of time with her, she has become a loving, contented horse with the help of her friend Charger. Age unknown.

CHARGER was adopted as a puppy, and has grown into a large, strong dog with a very happy disposition. Charger loved to go on walks with her best friend Sugar on a double leash. She also insisted on wearing sunglasses. Charger passed away peacefully in 2021 at the age of 12.

This sequel is dedicated to
the beautiful children, grand-children, cousins, nieces and nephews
that have all played an important part in its development.

Thanks to the loving support of this close-knit family
and the special bond between the author and the artist,
this book series is able to continue.

We would like to give special thanks to
the wonderful librarians of the Rancho Santa Fe Library
for their invaluable time, meticulous input and endless support.

Use these blank pages to draw any of your favorite characters.

www.ingramcontent.com/pod-product-compliance
Lightning Source LLC
Chambersburg PA
CBHW040405100426

42811CB00017B/1837